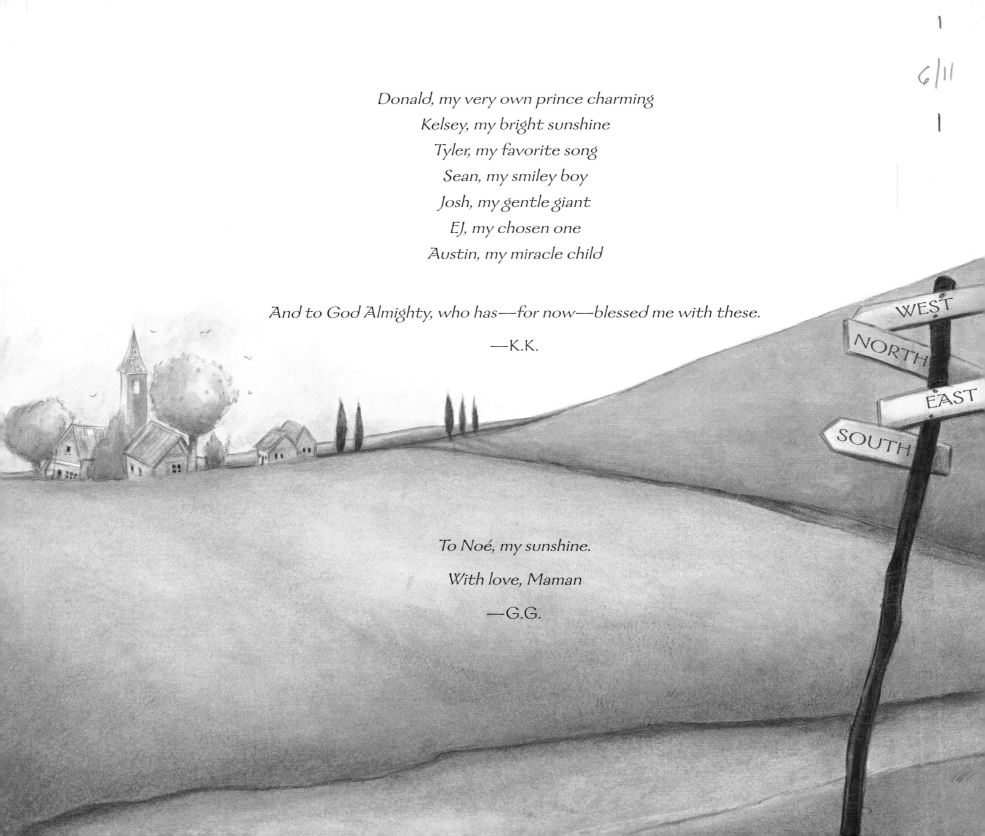

Donald, my very own prince charming

Kelsey, my bright sunshine

Tyler, my favorite song

Sean, my smiley boy

Josh, my gentle giant

EJ, my chosen one

Austin, my miracle child

And to God Almighty, who has—for now—blessed me with these.

—K.K.

To Noé, my sunshine.

With love, Maman

—G.G.

Brave Young Knight

WRITTEN BY

KAREN KINGSBURY

ILLUSTRATED BY

GABRIELLE GRIMARD

ZONDERkidz

ZONDERVAN.com/
AUTHORTRACKER
follow your favorite authors

ZONDERKIDZ

Brave Young Knight
Copyright © 2011 by Karen Kingsbury
Illustrations © 2011 by Gabrielle Grimard

Requests for information should be addressed to:
Zonderkidz, *Grand Rapids, Michigan 49530*

Library of Congress Cataloging-in-Publication Data

Kingsbury, Karen.
    Brave young knight / by Karen Kingsbury ; [illustrations by Gabrielle Grimard].
        p. cm.
    Summary: Although not the speediest, strongest, or most intelligent, a kind, honest knight
wins a bravery competition to become prince of the kingdom.
    ISBN 978-0-310-71645-7 (hardcover)
    [1. Conduct of life—Fiction. 2. Courage—Fiction. 3. Knights and knighthood—Fiction. 4.
Contests—Fiction.] I. Grimard, Gabrielle, ill. II. Title.
PZ7.K6117Br 2011
[E]—dc22   2008053938

Published in association with the literary agency of Alive Communications, Inc.,
7680 Goddard Street, Suite 200, Colorado Springs, CO 80920.
www.alivecommunications.com

Zonderkidz is a trademark of Zondervan.

Editor: Barbara Herndon
Art direction and design: Kris Nelson

Printed in China

10 11 12 13 14 15 /LPC/ 10 9 8 7 6 5 4 3 2 1

Show me your ways, O Lord,
teach me your paths;
guide me in your truth and teach me,
for you are God my Savior,
and my hope is in you all day long.

—Psalm 25:4-5

There once was a young knight who lived in a village on the west side of the kingdom. In the busy streets and cozy houses of the village everyone knew the young knight. He could run like the wind, carry a dog under each arm, and solve the toughest puzzles.

When the young knight passed by, people smiled and said, "Someday that knight will be named the best and bravest in the kingdom, and the west village will be honored."

One time, the young knight of the west village saw a woman carrying a load of bricks. The young knight hurried to her side. "Ma'am," he said, "may I carry your bricks?" Every day after that, the young knight met the woman at the brickyard and carried her bag of bricks until her house was built.

Another time, the bridge over the river washed away. The men in the west village puzzled over how much wood they would need to build a new bridge, but the young knight came up with a plan.

The men did as the knight said, and sure enough, they figured out exactly how many logs were needed to build a bridge across the river.

But the young knight of the west village was more than blazing fast, fiercely strong, and deeply intelligent. He was also kind. Once when the children were out playing, the young knight noticed a boy whose legs hadn't worked since he was born. "Boy," the knight said, "I can be your legs!" He put the boy on his shoulders and ran in circles and great arcs, and the wind whipped through the boy's hair. And they both laughed and laughed. The young knight was kind that way.

Now, the kingdom was made up of four villages—the west village, the east village, the north village, and the south village. The king announced that the bravest knight of the kingdom would be named prince, and everyone hoped a knight from their village would be chosen.

A knight from the east village was said to be so fast he could outrun his horse.

When the young knight from the west village heard about this, he practiced his running over and over again.

"I'm trying," he told his father. "but I'm not sure if I'm the fastest knight in the land."

His father smiled. "My son, the bravest knight is not always the fastest. Follow God and he will help you run the race."

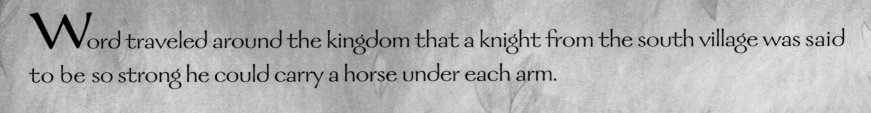

Word traveled around the kingdom that a knight from the south village was said to be so strong he could carry a horse under each arm.

When the young knight from the west village heard about this, he practiced lifting three dogs, then four dogs, then five. But he could never manage to lift his horse.

"I'm trying," he told his father. "But I'm not sure if I'm the strongest knight in the land."

Again his father smiled. "My son, the bravest knight is not always the strongest. Faith in God will give you the strength you need."

News made it through the kingdom that a knight from the north village was said to be so smart he could solve puzzles the village teachers couldn't solve.

When the young knight from the west village heard this, he solved every puzzle he could find. But he was never summoned by the village teachers to solve anything for them.

"I'm trying," he told his father. "But I'm not sure if I'm the smartest knight in the land."

His father smiled one more time. "My son, the bravest knight is not always the smartest. Ask God and he will give you great wisdom."

Soon the king called these four knights together. "I will stage a competition," the king said. "Bravery means many things. You will be tested in speed, strength, and intelligence. At the end of the competition, I will determine which of you is the bravest, the one who will be named prince of the kingdom."

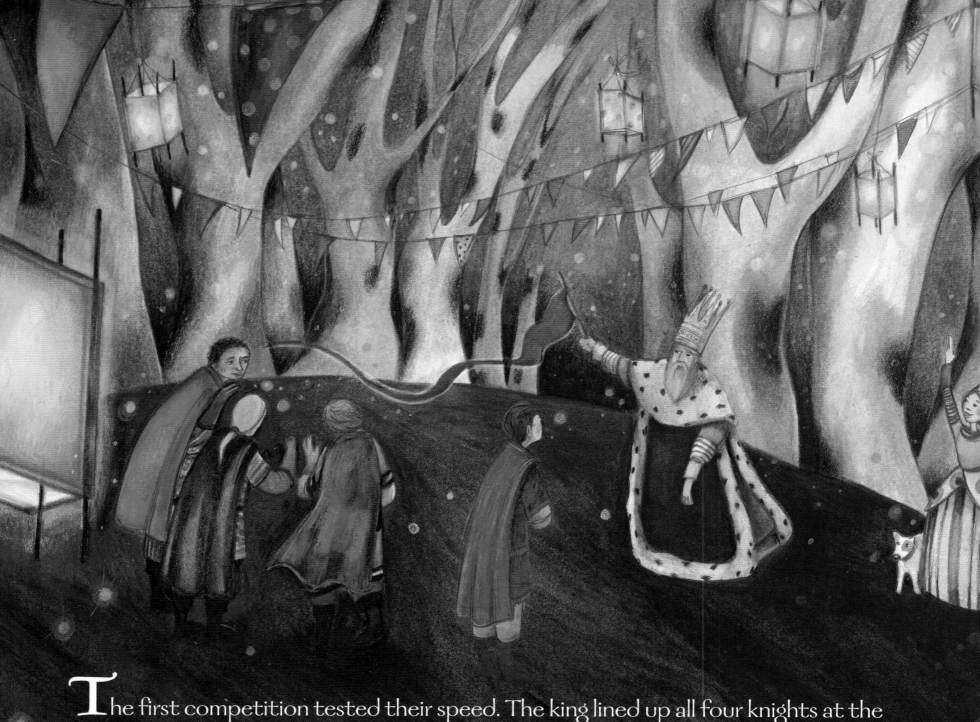

The first competition tested their speed. The king lined up all four knights at the entrance to the great and mighty forest. "Follow the course through the forest until you

A few minutes into the race, the knight from the east village shouted to the others, "I know a shortcut. Never mind the course marked out for us." He made a turn off the path and waved to the others. "Follow me."

And the knights from the south and north villages did just that.

But the young knight from the west village stayed the course and crossed the finish line long after the other three knights.

The second competition tested their strength. The king said, "In the lumberyard, find the biggest log you can carry from those I've set aside for you and bring it back to me."

When they reached the lumberyard, the knight from the south village pointed to a different pile of logs. "Some of these are hollow," he said. "We can carry much bigger logs if they are hollow." He nodded at the others. "Come on," he said. "Follow me." And the knights from the east and north villages did just that.

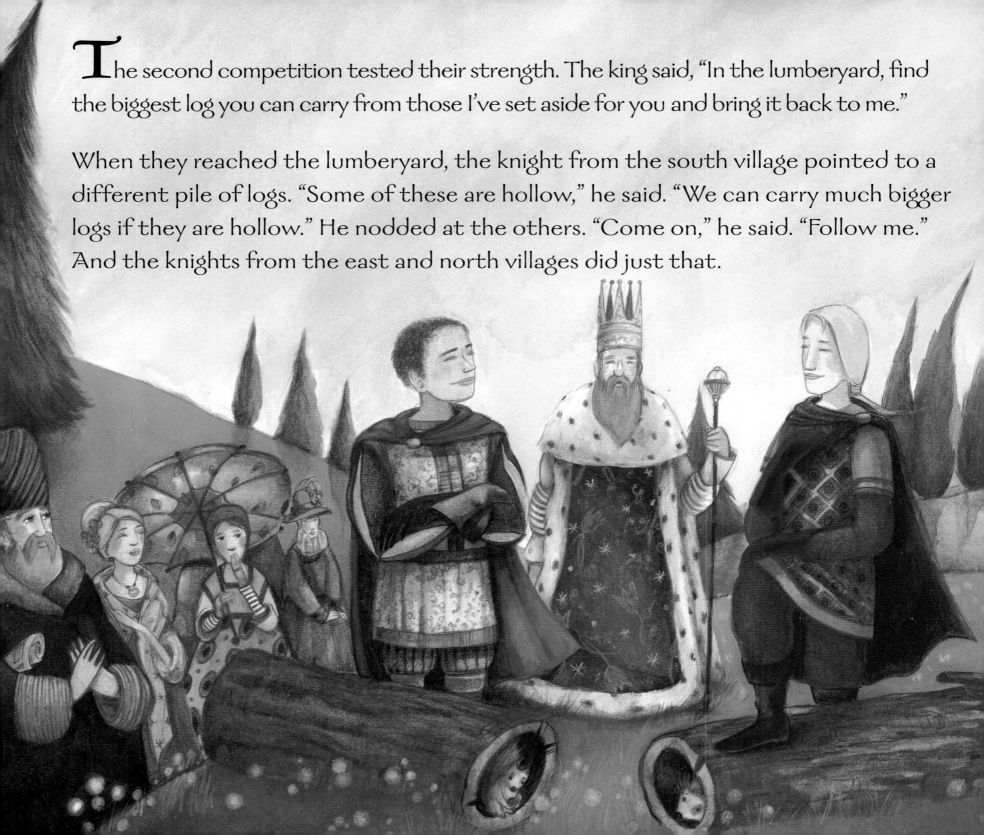

But the young knight from the west village found a medium-size log from among those the king had set aside. When he brought it back to the king, his was the smallest of all the logs. But it was solid.

The final competition tested intelligence. The king handed each of the knights a treasure map marked with different puzzles. "You must solve each puzzle along the way," the king told them. "Find your treasure and bring it to me."

When they'd each solved a few puzzles, the knight from the north village saw that the king was not around. "I know a man in town," he said, "who can give puzzle answers, ten for a dollar. This is your chance," he said as he began to run toward town. "Follow me."

And the knights from the east and south villages did just that.

But the young knight from the west village sat on a rock and figured out the puzzles, one at a time, as the king directed. When he finally found his treasure and brought it to the king, the treasures from the other three knights were already lined up near the throne.

Tallies were made by the king, and scores were analyzed. The knight from the east village was fastest. The knight from the south village was strongest, and the knight from the north village was smartest. The young knight from the west village thought he would never be named prince of the kingdom. The young knight saw his father in the crowd. His father smiled at him, and the young knight knew even if he didn't win the competition, his father loved him.

"I have decided on a winner," the king announced. And the people of the kingdom gathered around to hear.

The king looked at the knight from the east village. "You cheated by running off the course. You cannot be prince of the kingdom."

Next, the king turned to the knight from the south village. "You stole a hollow log from another pile of lumber. You cannot be prince of the kingdom."

Then the king spoke to the knight from the north village. "You lied about solving the puzzles, so you cannot be prince of the kingdom."

At last, the king spoke to the knight from the west village. "Well done! You were honest and finished the tasks as you were asked. You did not cheat, so you are the bravest knight of all."

So the brave young knight of the west village became prince and, with God's help, ruled the kingdom with character, kindness, and truth.

Because of the brave young knight, the kingdom became the strongest in the land, and the people of the west village were honored.

And they lived happily ever after.